WELCOME TO Pump Street Primary

Meet some of the children ...

Barry Barsby

Daisy Poborski

Rashid Ali

Floella Potts

Freddie Stanton

Monica Bellis

... in Miss Twigg's class

Craig Soapy

Karen Smart

Terry Flynn

Fatima Patel

Lily Wongsam

Paul Dimbley

Titles in the Pump Street Primary series

THIS IS BOB WILSON

He wrote this story
and drew the pictures.

He lives in the Derbyshire countryside in a house which he designed and built himself from an old cowshed. He has three grown-up children and nine grandchildren. When he was young he wanted to be a pop star, and he started to write songs. He became an art teacher and wrote plays and musicals, and shows for television and radio. Then he began to write and illustrate stories for children. He is the author of the *Stanley Bagshaw* picture books and the best-selling *Ging Gang Goolie, It's an Alien!*

First published 2000 by Macmillan Children's Books
a division of Macmillan Publishers Limited
25 Eccleston Place, London SW1W 9NF
Basingstoke and Oxford
www.macmillan.com

Associated companies throughout the world

ISBN 0 330 37092 8

3 5 7 9 8 6 4 2

A CIP catalogue record for this book is available from
the British Library.

Printed and bound in Great Britain by Mackays of Chatham plc, Kent

Visit Bob Wilson's website at www.planetbob.co.uk

written and illustrated by

Bob Wilson

MACMILLAN CHILDREN'S BOOKS

Here are some of the school staff ...

Mr C Warrilow BSc MEd

Miss Twigg

Mr Manley

Mr Boggis

Mrs York

Mr Lamp-Williams

Miss Gaters

Mrs Jellie

Norman Loops

Janice

Mrs Brazil

For Ami, Thomas, Elias,
Matilda, Reuben, Alexander,
Marius, Lucien and Babik

THIS IS DAISY POBORSKI

She looks quite a sensible sort of girl.

But she isn't.
Miss Twigg, our class teacher, says that
Daisy Poborski hasn't got the sense God
gave lettuce.

**Daisy! What on earth
are you doing with
those scissors?**

**Just looking to see if
they're sharp, Miss.**

When most children are asked to do a job they do it *carefully*.

I'm holding the sticky tape with both hands so I don't drop it, Miss.

That's very sensible, Lily.

And *thoughtfully*.

I've put the sponge on top of the cupboard where nobody can trip over it, Miss.

That's very thoughtful, Paul.

But Daisy has got what Miss Twigg
calls "an irresponsible attitude".
(I think she means she's a nutter.)
For example, last week Miss Twigg
said,

Daisy said,

Miss Twigg was not amused.

I don't think Daisy means to have an irresponsible attitude. She always does exactly as she is told.
For example, last Thursday at home time, Miss Twigg asked Daisy to put the chairs up on the tables and . . .

that's *exactly* what she did.

Miss Twigg didn't think it was funny.

One day last term a policeman came to give us a talk about Road Safety.
He told us about the dangers of playing in the street.

Then we practised doing the Green Cross Code.

Look right again.

The policeman was not amused. He said, "Some children don't seem to be taking this lesson very seriously . . . but they *should*."

Every single day a young girl gets knocked down by a car simply because she doesn't cross the road properly.

Crikey!

said Daisy.

Karen Smart (who's very clever)* said,

*At least she thinks she is.

And Miss Twigg burst out laughing.
But the policeman said that it was no
laughing matter. He said that he'd a
good mind to report someone.
Then Miss Twigg stopped laughing.

And she said it wasn't funny.
She said that it was *not funny at all*.
She said that Daisy Poborski had better
start to do something about her
irresponsible attitude, otherwise one of
these days she'd come to a sticky end.
And she did.
On Monday the 9th of May
at exactly 15 minutes past ten
Daisy Poborski came to a

Very
Very
Sticky
END!

THE SORT OF STICKY END THAT'S GOT FLOUR, SUGAR,
CHOCOLATE, EGGS AND . . . <u>MEGABLASTOHEXAPHENE</u> IN IT!

Miss Twigg asked us for our help. She said,

> Listen, everybody. I know something about the head teacher . . . and he doesn't know that I know.

> In seven days' time it will be his birthday. His 50th birthday.

Miss Twigg said she'd been thinking that it would be good if our class were to do something special for Mr Warrilow's fiftieth birthday.
But she had a problem.

The problem is, I can't for the life of me think what we could do.

"I know what we could do!" said Julie.

We could have a
DISCO PARTY!

I think Mr Warrilow might be getting a bit too old for disco dancing. Don't you, Julie?

It was only a suggestion,

said Julie.
Miss Twigg said that we should remember that Mr Warrilow would be *50 years old*. A fiftieth birthday was very special. She wondered if there was something that we could *make* Mr Warrilow.
Something which would make his birthday an unforgettable occasion.
"I know what we could make!" said Rashid.

We could make him a **BIRTHDAY CARD!**

"And we could write an unforgettable birthday message inside," said Barry. "Now, that's a good idea," said Miss Twigg.

What could the message say?

It's your BIRTHDAY ON TUESDAY SO DON'T FORGET (PS. Sorry about you being too OLD to go to Discos any more.)

What d'you think?

Miss Twigg thought about Barry's and
Rashid's birthday message. Then she
said, "On second thoughts I'm not sure
that sending Mr Warrilow a birthday
card would be such a good idea after
all."

Rashid said,  said Barry.

Miss Twigg said, "Now, listen everybody. Listen carefully to what I'm going to say. It might give you *food* for thought. Mr Warrilow is such a *sweet* man, I think he deserves a good *blow out* on his birthday, don't you?"

She said that with our *mixture* of talents we ought to be able to *cook up* a really big surprise. "Think about it," she said.

We all thought about it.

Then Daisy said, "I know, Miss – I've got it!"

"No, Daisy!" said Miss Twigg. "I didn't mean that sort of surprise. I meant a *nice* surprise."

Karen Smart (who knows everything about everybody)* said, "Mr Warrilow wouldn't enjoy having his ears banged, would he, Miss?"

* At least she thinks she does.

"What's a vegetarian?" said Daisy.

"A veg-et-arian," said Karen,

Just then Mrs Brazil, the school cook, popped her head round the door. She wanted to have a quick word with Miss Twigg – in private.
Miss Twigg went out into the corridor.

When she came back into the
classroom, Miss Twigg had a big
surprise.

"A birthday cake? What a brilliant
idea!" said Miss Twigg.

everybody in our class was very excited. Today we were going to help Miss Twigg bake a cake for Mr Warrilow's birthday. The cake was called

Italian
CHOCOLATE
SURPRISE

But before we started Miss Twigg had something very important to say. She said that cooking could be dangerous and that she was relying on us all to take care and behave sensibly.
Then she said, "Now, I'm going to give each of you a job to do. First, I need someone to *carefully* crack three eggs into a bowl."
"I could do that!" said Daisy.

Next, Miss Twigg needed someone to *very carefully* pour in half a cup of milk.
"I could do that too!" said Daisy.

Then she needed someone to *very carefully* and *very sensibly* measure out 170 grams of sugar.
"I'm absolutely brilliant at very carefully and sensibly measuring out 170 grams of sugar," said Daisy.
Soon everybody had been given a job.*

*Well, nearly everybody.

Miss Twigg hadn't forgotten about Daisy. She'd saved her for a special job. She said that when baking a cake "Timing" was very important. For example, the recipe said that the mixture should be whisked in a blender for three minutes.

"Leave it to me," said Daisy.

Then we were ready to begin. Karen
cracked the eggs into a bowl, Paul
poured in the milk, Julie added the
sugar. And everybody else did their jobs
– *carefully* and *sensibly*.
Miss Twigg started the blender.

Miss Twigg was not amused. She said,

"Daisy Poborski, just come down from there and stop being silly! And take care where you put your feet when you do. I don't want you knocking anything over. I wouldn't put it past you to spill soap powder into my cake mix. That really *would* give Mr Warrilow a surprise on his birthday."
And everybody laughed. (They thought Miss Twigg was joking.)

But she wasn't

"Don't worry, Miss," said Daisy.

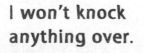

I won't knock anything over.

But she did!

Just then, Mr Boggis, who teaches the
Upper Juniors, popped his head round
the door.

"Oh yes," said Miss Twigg. "The
hymn for tomorrow's assembly. I
wondered . . ."
And she went out into the corridor to
have a word with Mr Boggis – in
private.
Which was unfortunate because that
meant she didn't see what Daisy did.
And so didn't realise what was going to
happen. Not until a bit later anyway.
By which time . . . IT WAS MUCH
TOO LATE!

When Miss Twigg came back into the room she was in a good mood again. "Right," she said. "Let's get cooking." She poured the cake mixture into a greased baking tin and put it in the oven.

Then she took her wristwatch off and gave it to Daisy.

The cake MUST come out of the oven at exactly quarter past ten.

Don't worry, Miss. I won't forget,

said Daisy.

After that we all went into the Art room and Miss Twigg told us what we were to do next.

I want you to design a pattern for the icing on the cake.

We were going to have a vote to choose the best design. When we'd all settled down and started to work, Miss Twigg said,

I'm just going next door to put away the cooking things.

when Miss Twigg decided to clean the
sink that she noticed something odd.
The scouring powder that should have
been on the shelf was on the floor.

And although it should have been
nearly full, it was nearly empty.

When she'd been training to be a
teacher she'd been given a very useful
book. It was called

A GUIDE FOR TRAINEE TEACHERS
(your questions answered)

Part 6: Safety in School

Q If a class of children are baking a cake for the head teacher's birthday what should a good teacher *always* do?

A The teacher should always make sure that one of the children doesn't accidently spill something dangerous such as scouring powder into the cake mixture.

Q What should a teacher do if she begins to suspect that one of the children already *has* spilled scouring powder into the cake mix?

A She should *start to worry*.

(If the scouring powder contains the active ingredient **Megablastohexaphene** she should really start to worry.)

We were all working quietly and sensibly when Miss Twigg came bursting in.

Daisy, I want a word with you.

I think Miss Twigg was going to say, "Daisy, you know when you climbed the shelves . . ." But Lily Wongsam said,

And I think she might also have said,
"Did you knock over a packet of . . ."
But Freddie Stanton said,

And all of a sudden, Miss Twigg didn't
say anything at all.

A GUIDE FOR TRAINEE TEACHERS
(your questions answered)

Q If a cake containing the active ingredient **MEGABLASTOHEXAPHENE** is put into a moderate oven and baked for 35 minutes what will happen?

A First of all someone will hear a funny rumbling noise.

Q Then what?

A Somebody will probably notice all the smoke coming from under the door.

Q Then what?

A The teacher in charge will almost certainly become speechless with terror.

Q Why?

A Because what will probably happen next is . . .

Nearly quarter past ten, Miss,

said Daisy.

"No, Daisy!" said Miss Twigg. "Don't go near that oven. Daisy, do you hear what I say? Come back here this minute! Whatever you do, don't open that oven door!"

Daisy, come back. You'll be blown to smithereens!

The explosion occurred at 10.15
precisely.
Mrs Jellie, the school secretary, had
been shut in her office since 8.57. She
had some important typing to do.
Pinned to her door was a notice.
It said

PLEASE DO NOT DISTURB
I have enough tribble working this
@£!?** computer as it is without
people bb*barging in and disrupting
me all the time.

She had been working very carefully
and methodically, and by 10.14 she'd
typed

and therefore, in view
of the seriousness of
this matter, and the
opinions expressed by
various members of the
governing body, the
chairman has asked me
to say

But at 10.15 *precisely* she typed . . .

Norman Loops, the school caretaker,
was in the entrance hall.

He was painting a sign ready for the Parents' Evening. He'd started work on it at ten past nine and had been working very quietly and carefully and thoughtfully.
By five minutes to ten he'd painted . . .

welcome

By ten past ten he'd painted . . .

o our

But at *exactly* quarter past ten he painted . . .

The little hand was on ten ... and the big hand was on two

In the hall, the infants were doing "Music and Movement" with Mrs York. Mrs York said,

> I want you to listen carefully to what I say, and watch very carefully what I do, then, when I've quite finished, I want you to do exactly the same.

The little hand
was on ten . . .

and the big hand
was on three

The infants listened very carefully to
what Mrs York said, and watched very
carefully what Mrs York did.

Then, when she was quite finished . . .

They did exactly the same.

Miss Twigg didn't shout or faint or fall off a ladder. She seemed to be in one of her thinking moods.
Fatima Patel said,

Please, Miss, where's Daisy gone?

Miss Twigg said nothing.
Paul Dimbley said,

Please, Miss, what's a smithereen?

Miss Twigg didn't reply.
Karen Smart said,

A smithereen is a little bit of something, Paul. So if someone is blown to smithereens it means . . .

Karen, for goodness sake, SHUT UP!

said Miss Twigg.
Then the door opened.

Cake's ready,

said Daisy.

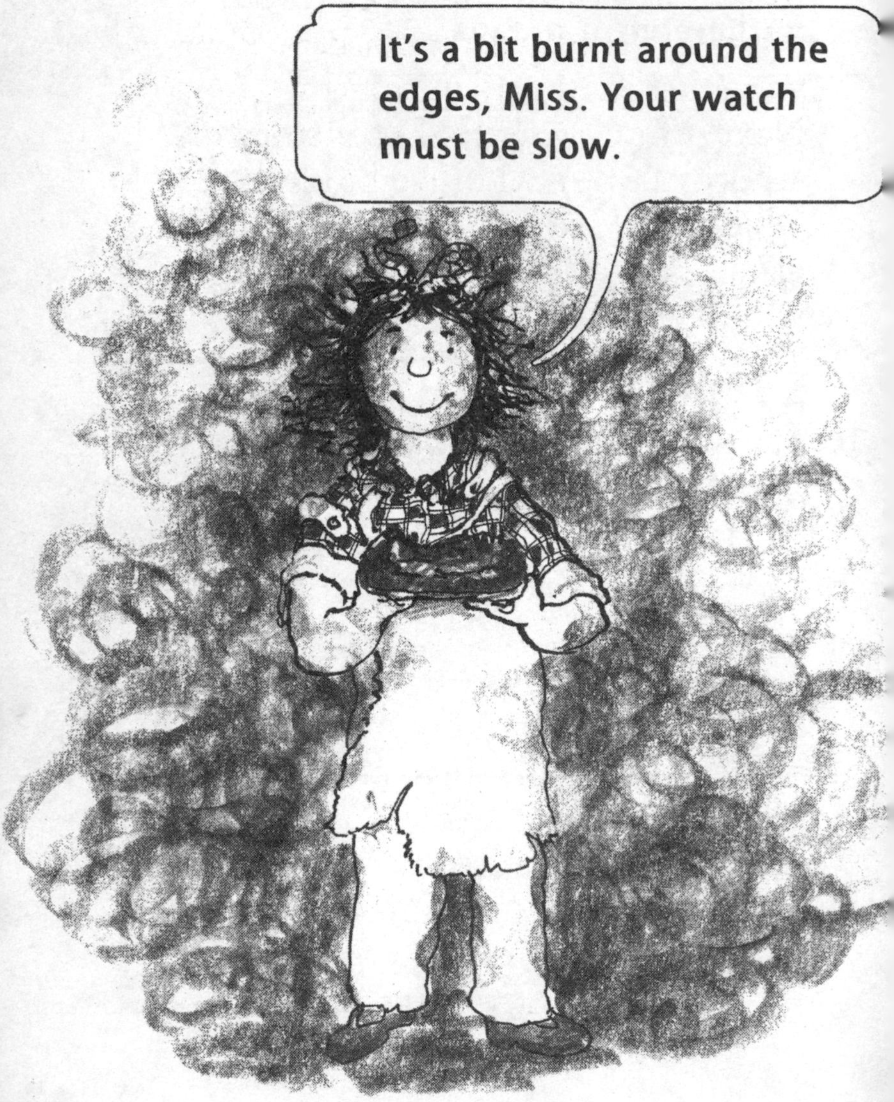
It's a bit burnt around the edges, Miss. Your watch must be slow.

we had assembly as usual. It was the
usual sort of assembly. First, Mr
Warrilow read out the notices. They
were the usual sort of notices.
Next, Miss Twigg told us a story about
an orphan boy who lived in India,
which was quite interesting. Then, as
usual, she told us the moral of the story,
which was quite boring.
Then Mr Warrilow, as usual, announced
the hymn.
But when Mr Boggis went over to the
piano he winked at Miss Twigg. And
when he started to play he didn't play
"All things bright and beautiful". He
played a different tune.
And Miss Twigg started singing it.
And the other teachers started singing.
And we all got the idea and we joined
in.
And Mrs Jellie and Norman Loops
and the dinner ladies joined in
until everybody in the whole
            school was singing

♪ Happy Birtha
Happy Birtha
Happy Birthday
♪ Happy Birtha

Mr Warrilow was completely taken by surprise. He didn't know what to say. He was absolutely speechless.

He said, "Well, I really don't know what to say. I'm absolutely stunned. Words escape me. I'm absolutely delighted. I'm truly dumbfounded. What a wonderful surprise. I didn't think anybody knew. I really am absolutely speechless."

Mr Warrilow might have said quite a bit more about how he couldn't think of anything to say but before he could say anything else at all . . . somebody else said,

said Daisy.

This time Mr Warrilow really was
speechless.
But Miss Twigg wasn't lost for words.
She said, "Oh my sainted aunt! Daisy,
you didn't bake that cake, did you?"

said Daisy.
And Miss Twigg smiled with relief.

But then she had a sudden thought!
"Daisy," she said. "You didn't by any
chance *help* your mother to bake the
cake, did you?"
"No," said Daisy.

And Miss Twigg smiled again. But she
stopped smiling when Daisy said,

Mr Warrilow wanted to know how Daisy had managed to make a candle all by herself.

"Well," said Daisy, "I melted lots of candle-ends into a bowl and stirred for exactly three minutes. But the mixture didn't look a very nice colour . . ."

"Splendid," said Mr Warrilow. "I'll light it now then, shall I?"

Right, everybody. Are you ready?

"NO!" said Miss Twigg. "That's really not a good idea . . ."

"One . . ." said Mr Warrilow.

"You see, that blue powder might have been Megablasto . . ."

"Two . . ." said Mr Warrilow.

"*Mr Warrilow*!" shouted Miss Twigg. "Whatever you do . . ."

Don't light
THAT CANDLE!

But he did!

THE END

BARRY'S BEAR

When Miss Twigg takes her class on a trip to a nature park she doesn't expect the wildlife to be quite so wild.

It was HUGE and HAIRY and very, very SCARY!

And it ate my strawberry yoghurt.

FLYING FLO

Flo is the smallest girl in her class. But that doesn't stop her having big ideas. Miss Twigg says she'll go a long way.

And at the school fête she nearly does.

I think she's heading in the general direction of China.

FOOTBALL FRED

Fred's a dancer, not a goalie. When Miss Twigg picks him for the match against St Mildred's, he says

I'll do the best I can, Miss.

But will Fred's best be good enough?

YES!

MONICA'S MONSTER

Miss Twigg likes animals. But when Monica brings little Samantha to school and says

Please, Miss, would you like to see my pet?

Miss Twigg says

NO!

PUMP STREET PRIMARY
titles available from Macmillan

1. Dangerous Daisy	0 330 37092 8	£3.50
2. Barry's Bear	0 330 37090 1	£3.50
3. Flying Flo	0 330 37094 4	£3.50
4. Football Fred	0 330 37091 X	£3.50
5. Monica's Monster	0 330 37093 6	£3.50
6. Rashid's Rescue	0 330 37095 2	£3.50

All Macmillan titles can be ordered at your local bookshop
or are available by post from:

Book Service by Post
PO Box 29, Douglas, Isle of Man IM99 1BQ

Credit cards accepted. For details:
Telephone: 01624 675137
Fax: 01624 670923
E-mail: bookshop@enterprise.net

Free postage and packing in the UK.
Overseas customers: add £1 per book (paperback)
and £3 per book (hardback).

The prices shown below are correct at the time of going to press.
However, Macmillan Publishers reserve the right to show new retail
prices on covers which may differ from those previously advertised.